CW01082054

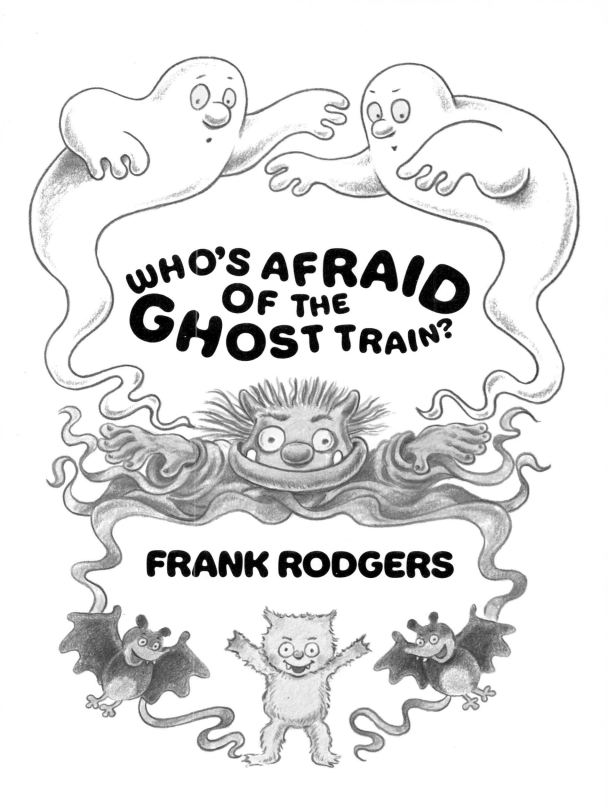

WHO'S AFRAID OF THE GHOST TRAIN?

FRANK RODGERS

PUFFIN BOOKS

For Zoë and Adam

Robert's house was a perfectly ordinary sort of house. But Robert thought it was full of scary things. He had a big imagination.

He was sure there was a dragon in the hall . . .

a steam train in the kitchen . . .

a thing that lived down the toilet . . .

a shark in the bath . . .

bears in the wardrobe . . .

and little men under his bed.

Robert's pals teased him about his big imagination. "Look out!" they shouted. "There's a cross-eyed, nine-legged, furry, flying monster behind you! Run!"

Robert was sure he could feel its big toe brushing against his leg.
So he ran.

Round the corner he met his Grandpa
Jim. "Help! I'm being chased by a
monster!" yelled Robert.
Grandpa Jim looked around.
"Nobody there, Robert," he said.
"Maybe you just imagined it, eh?"

"Why don't you do what I did when
I was a lion-tamer in the circus?"
"What was that?" asked Robert.

"The lions and tigers were as fierce as your monster," said Grandpa Jim, "but I just imagined they were like big babies and it helped me not to feel scared."
"That was clever, Grandpa," said Robert.

"You can do the same," said Grandpa Jim, "the next time you meet some monsters. It's easy!"
Robert laughed. "OK, Grandpa," he said, "I'll try it!"

Next day the funfair arrived in town and Robert and his friends went along. They stopped in front of the Ghost Train. FRIGHTS, THRILLS, SCREAMS, SHOCKS, it said. "Brilliant!" said Robert's friends. "Let's go in!"

They turned to Robert and laughed. "Want to see some *real* monsters, Robert?"
To their surprise Robert nodded his head. "All right," he said, "let's."

Inside the Ghost Train it was scary and eerie and very, very dark. Something tugged at their sleeves. Was it the horrible, warty old witch?

Cold, wet things brushed their faces. "EEEEK! It must have been the clammy fingers of the slimy monsters! It must have been!"

A grinning skeleton rattled his bones at them and a white ghost wailed in the shadows. WOOOOOOOOOOOOOOOOOO!
"Yaaaaaaaaaaaa!" yelled Robert's friends. "Let us out!"

But Robert just grinned. "Why?" he asked, "I'm enjoying myself."
"But what about your big imagination?" his friends said.

"I'm using it," replied Robert. "Imagine what these ghosts would look like first thing in the morning!"

Robert laughed, because there's nothing as funny as a monster trying to be scary in his vest and underpants!

Back outside, Robert's pals shuddered like jellies. "Ooer, that was horrible," they said.

Robert laughed. "So, you were scared after all?"

"No we weren't! Not a bit of it!" they yelled. "In fact, we'd like to see those scary old monsters again, we would!"

That gave Robert an idea. He opened his eyes and mouth wide
and pointed behind them. "Ooer," he gulped. "Yikes," he gasped.

"Look out!" shouted Robert. "The Ghost Train Monsters have escaped! They're coming after you . . . RUN!" Robert's friends heard something behind them, so they ran.

"My goodness," smiled Robert, "my friends have really big imaginations!"

"Just like me!"

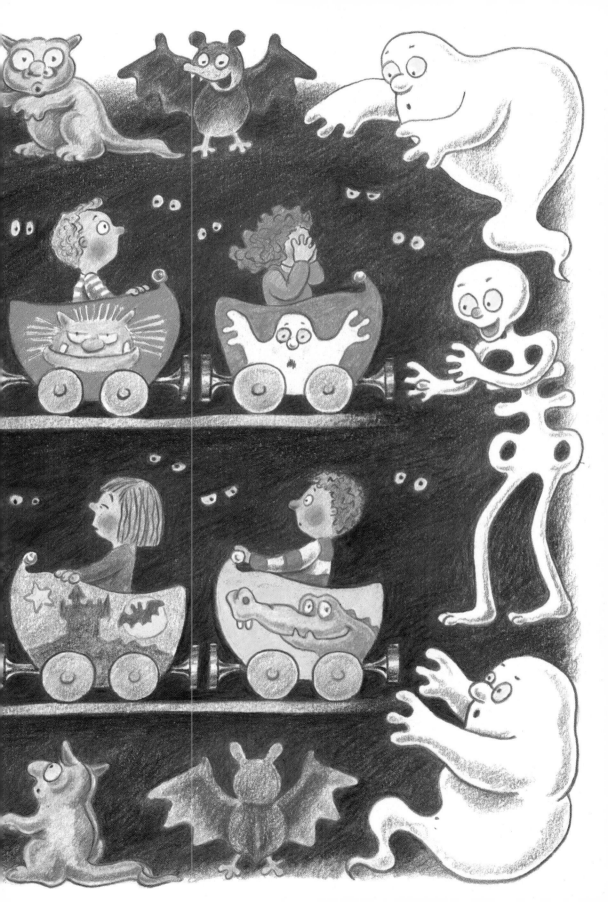